Science Matters

CLOUDS

Christine Webster

Published by Weigl Publishers Inc.
350 5th Avenue, Suite 3304, PMB 6G
New York, NY USA 10118-0069
Website: www.weigl.com

Library of Congress Cataloging-in-Publication Data

Webster, Christine.
Clouds / by Christine Webster.
p. cm. -- (Science matters)
Includes bibliographical references and index.
ISBN 1-59036-411-2 (alk. paper) -- ISBN 1-59036-417-1 (pbk. : alk. paper)
1. Clouds--Juvenile literature. I. Title. II. Series.
QC921.35.W43 2007
551.57'6--dc22
2005029918

Printed in the China
1 2 3 4 5 6 7 8 9 10 09 08 07 06

Editor Frances Purslow
Design and Layout Terry Paulhus

Cover: White, fluffy, cumulous clouds usually form below 6,000 feet (1830 meters) in the atmosphere.

Photograph Credits
University of Heidelberg, ESA: page 12T; **NASA, ESA, M. Robberto (Space Telescope Science Institute/ESA) and the Hubble Space Telescope Orion Treasury Project Team plus C.R. O'Dell (Rice University), and NASA:** pages 12 & 13 background; **NASA, ESA, J. Hester and A. Loll (Arizona State University):** page 14L; **Anthony Del Genio**: page 19.

Contents

Studying Clouds

Earth's atmosphere is always on the move. Great swirls of clouds dance across water and land, and then disappear. Each cloud is unique. Some are large and fluffy. Others are small and wispy. Some are white, while others are gray or black. The shape and color of a cloud tell us what kind of weather is coming.

Clouds are collections of tiny droplets of water or ice. They are important to life on this planet. Clouds act like a blanket to trap heat on Earth. They also protect Earth from too much sunshine.

Without clouds, there would be no rain or snow to water the land.

Cloud Facts

Did you know that fog is a cloud that hangs at ground level? Below are more interesting facts about clouds.

- Some storm clouds release as much energy as an **atomic bomb**.
- Most days, more than half of Earth's surface is covered by clouds.
- Airplanes can make their own clouds. They are formed from water vapor that is pushed out of the plane's engine.
- Earth is not the only planet with clouds. Mars, Jupiter, Saturn, Uranus, Neptune, and Pluto all have clouds. Some of their moons do, too.

How Clouds Form

Clouds are part of the **water cycle**. Every day, the Sun heats Earth. This heat turns water from our oceans, lakes, and rivers into a gas called water vapor. The water vapor then rises into the air. As it rises, it cools. The cooled water vapor **condenses** around tiny specks of dust in the air. These water droplets then crowd together to form clouds. When a cloud cannot hold any more moisture, it drops some of its moisture as rain, snow or ice. Then the water cycle begins again.

The water cycle uses Earth's water over and over.

Cloud Color

Clouds are not always white. They can also be gray or black. On sunny days, clouds are white and fluffy. On rainy days, clouds appear thick and gray.

The color of clouds is determined by the amount of water droplets or ice crystals in them. The droplets and crystals block the light. Dark clouds contain more moisture than white clouds.

Flat, dark clouds drop rain or snow. Tall, black clouds usually mean stormy weather. They often bring lightning and thunder with them. A rainstorm with strong winds is on its way. Sometimes there is hail.

Classifying Clouds

Just like snowflakes, no two clouds are alike. However, clouds can be grouped into four main types. Their names describe their appearance. The first type is cumulus, which means "piled up" in Latin. The next type is stratus, which means "layered." Cirrus is the third type. It means "wisps of hair." The final type is nimbus, which means "rain storm."

These names can also be combined. For example, "stratus" combined with "cumulus" make the word "stratocumulus." A stratocumulus cloud is layered and piled up. Likewise, cumulonimbus clouds are piled up clouds that produce thunderstorms.

Cirrus clouds are sometimes called "mare's tails."

Cloud Heights

Each type of cloud occurs at a certain height in the atmosphere. Some clouds are high, some are low, and some occur at medium height.

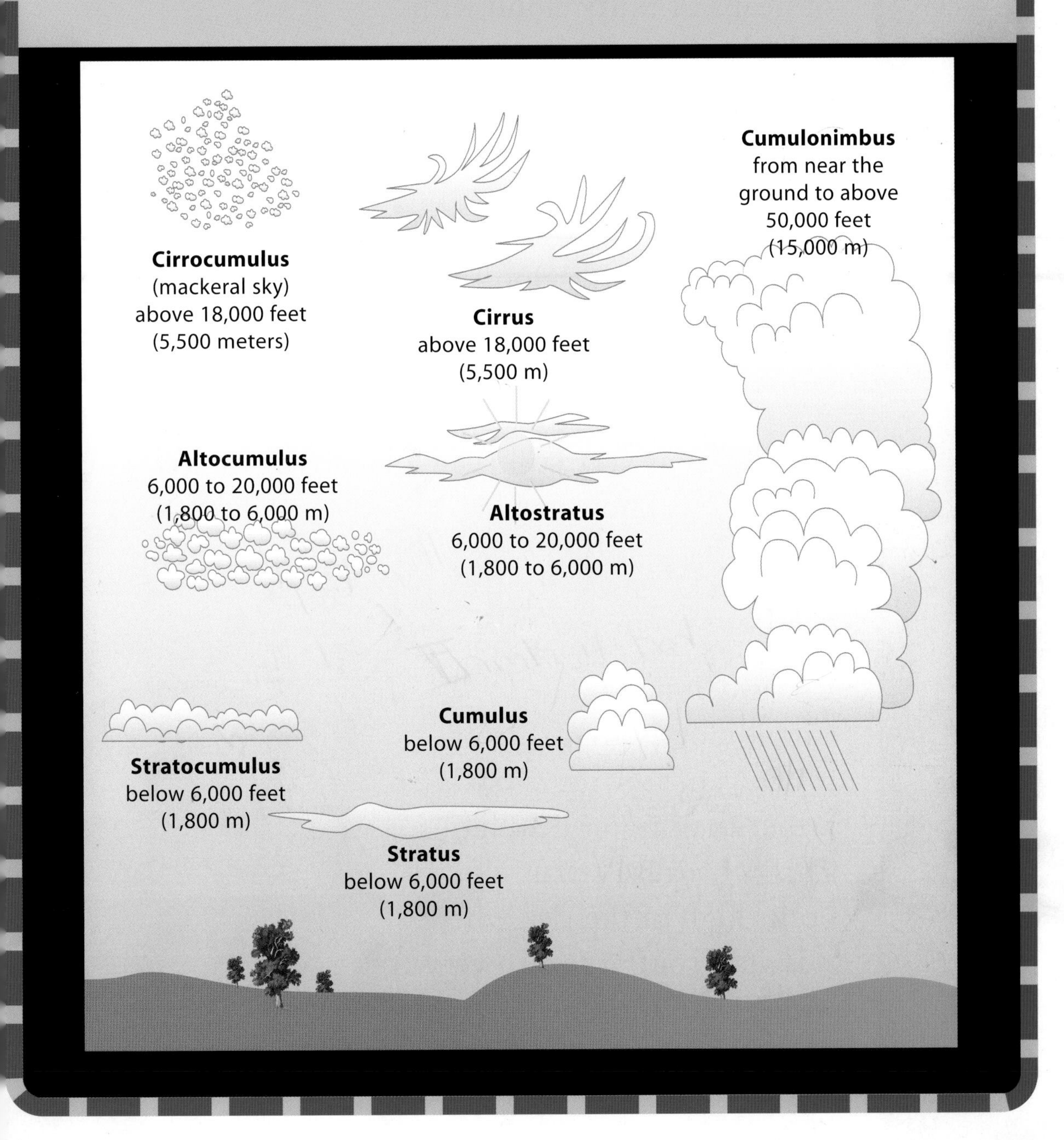

Cloud Types

Cumulus Clouds

The cumulus cloud looks like popcorn in the sky. It is made of heaps of fluffy cloud with a flat bottom.

Stratus Clouds

Stratus clouds appear as layers of unbroken clouds with a flat base. Sometimes they are so thin, the Sun is not blocked at all. They barely move because the air beneath them is very still. The lowest type of stratus cloud is known as fog.

Cirrus Clouds

Cirrus clouds are made of millions of tiny ice crystals rather than water droplets. This is because cirrus clouds occur high in the sky, where it is very cold. It is also very windy. The wind gives these clouds their wispy appearance.

Forecasting Weather

The type of clouds in the sky suggests what sort of weather is on the way.

A **Stratus** clouds bring light rain or snow.

B **Cumulus** clouds mean pleasant weather.

C **Cumulonimbus** clouds bring thunderstorms, heavy rains, or hail.

D **Cirrus** clouds mean that the weather is about to change.

Sky Technology

Geographic Information System (GIS)
Special computers called Geographic Information Systems (GIS) gather information about Earth. Scientists use GIS to map **air pollution** in cities and towns. Results are posted on the Internet so people can read about the types and amount of pollution where they live.

Telescopes
Telescopes help us see objects that are far away. Astronomers use them to observe space objects, such as stars, planets, and whole **galaxies**. Telescopes make distant objects appear closer by collecting light. Telescopes can collect more light than the human eye can.

Weather Satellite
Weather satellites are spacecraft that circle Earth. They provide a weather watch on the entire planet. Weather satellites take photographs of Earth's atmosphere. These help meteorologists predict storms and other weather patterns. These satellites also carry special instruments that record information on computers. They monitor events in the atmosphere, such as auroras, dust storms, pollution, and cloud systems.

Radar
Meteorologists gather huge amounts of information in order to predict the weather. **Radar** can tell them what is inside a cloud. This can be rain or hail. Radar can also track a storm that is coming. It helps meteorologists warn people if the storm is dangerous.

Storm Clouds

Sometimes a fluffy, white cumulus cloud turns into a cumulonimbus cloud. This type of cloud is tall and dark. It is sometimes called a thundercloud. The flat bottom hangs low in the sky, but its top spreads high into the atmosphere. A cumulonimbus cloud brings stormy weather. It can bring hail, thunder, and lightning. It can even bring a tornado.

Storm clouds bring needed moisture to dry areas, such as the plains in Texas.

Lightning and Thunder

It is very windy inside a cumulonimbus cloud. The wind rubs ice particles and raindrops together. This rubbing creates electric sparks, much like when you rub your feet on a wool carpet on a dry day.

Electric sparks created in thunderclouds are huge. They leap through the sky as lightning bolts. Lightning is so hot that it expands and splits the air it travels through. This sudden movement of large air masses causes shock waves, which are heard as thunder. Since light travels faster than sound, we see lightning before we hear it.

Protecting Earth

Clouds are important to life on Earth. Clouds protect Earth from the Sun's rays. Too much sunshine would **evaporate** all of Earth's water. As part of the water cycle, clouds bring moisture from the oceans and drop it on dry land as rain and snow. After watering the land, this moisture again fills up the rivers, lakes, and oceans. As well, the water droplets in clouds trap the heat and keep the planet warm. Clouds also protect people from some of the Sun's rays. These rays are harmful to people's skin.

Clouds provide water for thirsty crops, animals, and people.

Cloud Seeding

Earth needs moisture. Sometimes an area does not receive enough moisture. A cloud passing over such an area can be seeded with special particles to make it rain on the dry area. This is called cloud seeding.

For a cloud to release rain, tiny water droplets must join together to form bigger, heavier drops of water. Natural raindrops form when water vapor condenses on dust or salt in the air. Cloud seeding provides the specks on which the droplets form. The chemical silver iodide is released into the cloud from attachments on the wings of an airplane. Moisture clings to the particles of silver iodide and falls as rain. Silver iodide also prevents large hailstones from forming and destroying farmers' crops.

Pollution and Clouds

Not all clouds are gentle and fluffy. Some clouds are filled with bad things. Smoke from fires and factories adds chemicals to the air. So does exhaust from cars and trucks. In large amounts, these chemicals can harm the environment. They can create air pollution. Water vapor in the air can cling to these chemicals and form clouds. These polluted water droplets become a weak acid. They fall to the ground as **acid rain**. Acid rain kills plants and poisons drinking water. It can even **corrode** statues and buildings.

The trees in the "Black Triangle," a highly polluted area in the Czech Republic, are heavily damaged by acid rain.

A Life of Science

Dr. Anthony Del Genio

Dr. Anthony Del Genio is an **atmospheric scientist**. He works at NASA's Goddard Institute of Space Studies. Dr. Del Genio studies clouds to forecast how the climate might change in the future. He has studied questions such as:
If **global warming** does occur, how severe will it be?
If Earth's oceans warm up, will more clouds form?
How would this affect Earth's climate?

Dr. Del Genio studies weather conditions using information from satellites and from instruments on Earth. He also examines weather conditions on other planets. Dr. Del Genio noticed that many weather patterns on Saturn look like those on Earth. Perhaps this information will help scientists predict Earth's future weather patterns.

Surfing Cloud Science

How can I find more information about clouds?

- Libraries have lots of interesting books on clouds.
- The Internet has some great websites dedicated to clouds.

Where can I find a good reference website to learn more about clouds?

Encarta Homepage
www.encarta.com

- Type "clouds" into the search engine.
- Other terms to try are "stratus," "cirrus," or "cumulus."

How can I find out more about clouds?

Science for Families
www.scienceforfamilies.allinfo-about.com

- For cloud activities, type "clouds" into the search engine.

Plymouth State Meteorology Program
http://vortex.plymouth.edu/clouds.html

- Click on links to see pictures of various types of clouds.

Science in Action

Make Your Own Cloud

Using the water cycle, you can make your own cloud.

You will need:

- warm water
- a jar
- a metal dish
- a fridge or freezer

Place the metal dish into the freezer for about an hour.

Put about an inch (2.5 centimeters) of warm water into a jar.

Remove the metal dish from the freezer and place it on top of the jar.

What happened inside the jar?

Can you explain the process?

What Have You Learned?

1. Name three things that can fall from a cloud.

2. What type of clouds look like wisps of hair?

3. What does a cumulonimbus cloud tell us?

4. Why are clouds sometimes seeded?

5. What are clouds made of?

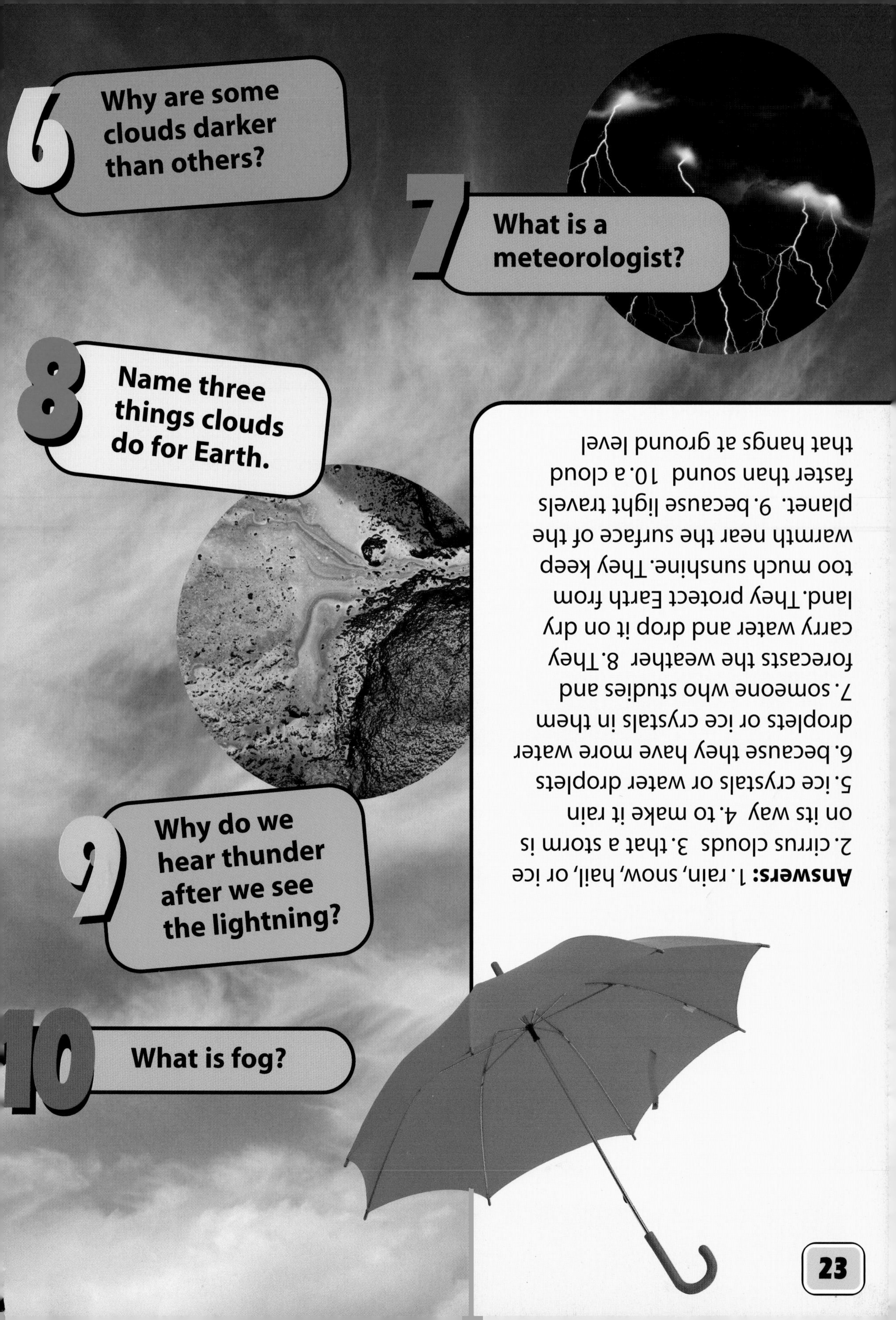

6 Why are some clouds darker than others?

7 What is a meteorologist?

8 Name three things clouds do for Earth.

9 Why do we hear thunder after we see the lightning?

10 What is fog?

Answers: 1. rain, snow, hail, or ice 2. cirrus clouds 3. that a storm is on its way 4. to make it rain 5. ice crystals or water droplets 6. because they have more water droplets or ice crystals in them 7. someone who studies and forecasts the weather 8. They carry water and drop it on dry land. They protect Earth from too much sunshine. They keep warmth near the surface of the planet. 9. because light travels faster than sound 10. a cloud that hangs at ground level

Words to Know

acid rain: rain that has become a weak acid by mixing with air pollution

air pollution: harmful materials, such as gases and chemicals, that make air dirty

atmospheric scientist: someone who studies Earth's atmosphere

atomic bomb: a bomb that splits atoms to cause a huge explosion

condenses: changes from a gas to a liquid by cooling

corrode: dissolve or wear away

evaporate: change from a liquid to a gas

galaxies: large groups of stars

global warming: a theory that Earth's atmosphere is slowly warming

radar: a system that uses radio waves to locate objects in the atmosphere

water cycle: the circular trip water takes from Earth's surface to the sky and back to Earth again

Index